YL

The New Dress

For the wee boy in Hans Christian Andersen's
The Emperor's New Clothes – IC

For Jill – CM

1 3 5 7 9 10 8 6 4 2

Copyright © text Ivor Cutler 1995

Copyright © illustrations Claudio Muñoz 1995

Ivor Cutler and Claudio Muñoz have asserted their rights under
the Copyright, Designs and Patents Act, 1988 to be identified as
the author and illustrator of this work

First published in the United Kingdom 1995
by The Bodley Head Children's Books
Random House, 20 Vauxhall Bridge Road, London SW1V 2SA

Random House Australia (Pty) Limited
20 Alfred Street, Milsons Point, Sydney,
New South Wales 2061, Australia

Random House New Zealand Limited
18 Poland Road, Glenfield,
Auckland 10, New Zealand

Random House South Africa (Pty) Limited
PO Box 337, Bergvlei 2012, South Africa

Random House UK Limited Reg. No. 954009

A CIP catalogue record for this book is available from the British Library

ISBN 0 370 31873 0

Designed by Rowan Seymour

Printed in China

The New Dress

Ivor Cutler

Illustrated by Claudio Muñoz

The Bodley Head
London

The New Dress

Allegro   © Ivor Cutler 1994

f Hooray! Hooray!

I'm going to wear my dress,

But first of all I'll have to don

My socks and pants and vest.

Jelly sat on her sandal and looked up at Mum.
  'I'd like a new dress,' she frowned.
  'Make one yourself,' said Mrs Haystack, stirring a huge
pot of Scotch broth.

'How do you make them?' asked Jelly, scratching an itchy place on her back and standing up.

'You cut a piece of cloth the shape of the front of a dress, then you cut a piece of cloth the shape of the back of a dress, then you sew them together,' said Mum. 'Use these kitchen scissors, and there's a piece of cloth on top of my chest-of-drawers.' She stooped.

Jelly kissed her lips, wiped the scissors on the dish towel and ran into the bedroom.

There, on top of the chest-of-drawers, lay a lovely piece of soft canvas. She climbed on a chair and pressed the canvas to her face to sniff its strong, fresh smell.

Then she brought the fabric down, along with a comb, a hairbrush, a box of paper hankies, a dozen hairgrips, a bottle of handcream and a pink plastic sack of cotton-wool balls.

'Mum,' she called, 'you never told me to be careful.'

'Be careful with those scissors, Jelly,' called back Mrs Haystack, 'they're very sharp – and the points are very sharp too, like number seven needles.'

'What's a number seven needle, Mum?' asked Jelly.

'This is,' whispered her mum, digging her fingers into her daughter's ribs.

'You'll tickle me to death,' screamed Jelly. 'I know what a number seven needle is now.'

'Good!' said Mrs Haystack, and returned to the soup.

Jelly cut out a front, then she cut out a back and placed it on top of the front, then she snipped bits off till the front and the back were both the same.

In the big basket lay a large needle and a ball of orange wool. Jelly sucked the wool and made a point, then threaded it. She sewed the back to the front.

'Here it is, Mum,' she called and took it through to the kitchen.

'Slip it on and let me see,' said her mother.

Jelly pulled her dress off and tried to pull the canvas one on. It wouldn't budge.

'Here let me see,' said her mother and held the dress up to have a look.

'Jelly,' she shook her head. 'You forgot to leave holes for your head,' she touched her girl's head; 'and your arms,' she slid her hands down Jelly's arms; 'and your legs. Just snip the wool here and here and here and here and here and here and here and here.'

The telephone rang so Jelly went back to the bedroom, snipped where Mum had said and drew out the superfluous pieces of wool. She pulled on the dress and stood before the mirror, thinking.

'Mum, this dress needs decorating,' she called and stepped into the kitchen.

'The Binks can't come for supper,' said Mum. 'Oh, my poor Scotch broth!'

Jelly threw her arms round her mother to comfort her. 'I know,' she said, 'we can decorate my dress with it.'

Mrs Haystack sat up and burst out laughing. 'Gelignite Haystack, you're a genius.'

They looked at the broth. There were peas and carrots and
barley and leeks and new turnips and red lentils.

Mum lifted the strainer from the hook, fetched out the
vegetables and spread them on a metal tray. 'Wait till
they're cool, Jelly, then decorate your dress.'

Jelly smoothed gum over the front. When she had finished, she bent over the tray of vegetables and felt them: nice and cool. She placed the tray by the dress and went to work, spreading handfuls of vegetables all over till the dress was covered. Then she carefully turned over the dress and did the same to the back; first the gum and then the vegetables.

She slipped the dress on. It felt as heavy as a pig. 'Look, Mum. My new dress!' she called and staggered into the kitchen.

Mrs Haystack walked round Jelly making quiet noises like 'ts ts' and 'hm hm'.

Then she stepped forward, put her fingers under the shoulders and lifted.

'Jelly, this weighs a ton,' she said, and let the dress drop.

Jelly sat down suddenly on the floor.

'You know, dear, most of this weight is water. Let's hang it out on the line to dry.'

They stepped outside and pegged the dress to the line. It was so heavy that they had to use the clothes pole to raise it off the grass, and the pole even bent a bit. Then they went inside to eat their soup.

While they ate, Mrs Haystack gave Jelly words to spell. Jelly loved spelling and only got one word wrong.

'The birds are busy out there,' said Jelly. 'Listen to all those wings.'

'I expect they are going back to their nests for the night. Shall we step outside and test the dress?' asked her mother.

'Finished,' gasped Jelly. 'That was lovely soup.' She laid down her spoon and left the table.

When they went out,
hundreds of birds flew off,
like a breeze, leaving the air
full of floating feathers.

'Mum,' said Jelly in a
small voice, clutching her big
warm hand, 'look at my
dress! The birds ate it!'

'They must have thought it was a present,' said Mrs
Haystack.

She snatched the gummy dress from the line and handed
it to Jelly. 'Quick, round the garden and catch the feathers
on your dress, while I run your bath,' said Mum.

Jelly raced three times round the garden, then went
straight into the house and donned her new feather dress.

She gazed at the mirror in delight then ran into the bathroom.

'Beautiful!' sighed her mother. 'We'll go shopping in it tomorrow and drop in at the Binks'.'

Then she pulled her daughter's clothes off and dumped her
in the bath with a splash.